MUSIC and DRUM
Voices of War and Peace, Hope and Dreams

poems selected by LAURA ROBB

illustrated by DEBRA LILL

When men turn mob
Drums throb;
When mob turns men
Music again.

Archibald MacLeish
excerpt from *Music and Drum*

PHILOMEL BOOKS

From where the sun now stands
I will fight no more forever

War

Hear me, my warriors: my heart is sick and sad.

Our chiefs are killed,

The old men are all dead.

It is cold, and we have no blankets;

The little children are freezing to death.

Hear me, my warriors: my heart is sick and sad.

From where the sun now stands I will fight no more forever!

Chief Joseph of the Nez Percé Tribe
(spoken on his defeat in 1877)

A War Game

A crippled soldier
returning from a menagerie
that the newspapers called
war

A crippled soldier
crying in hands
that spilled the blood
of children
   of laughing, weeping children
Even some children
that dressed up
in horrible suits,
with guns and bombs,
to play a fatally
unhappy game

Allan Richards

Little Song of the Maimed

Lend me your arm
to replace my leg
The rats ate it for me
at Verdun
at Verdun
I ate lots of rats
but they didn't give me back my leg
and that's why I was given the *Croix de Guerre*
and a wooden leg
and a wooden leg

Benjamin Peret
translated from the French by David Gascoyne

The Friend I Met While Running from the War

He went away,
his father carrying him piggyback,
following the brook
where the clouds rush noisily by,
the friend I met while running from the war.

When the cannons' roar
came over the mountain ridge,
the cicadas stopped singing
and there was only the barking of the dog
keeping watch alone
in the house of camellias
behind the garden walls.

We would take turns eating
mouthfuls of wild strawberries
and share green apples,
the friend whose name I never knew,
running from the war.

In June,
my friend's face
rises
in the clouds of flowers.

Dearer than a hometown friend,
I haven't heard from him since,
the friend I met while running from the war.

Song Myŏng-ho
translated from the Korean by Ann Sung-hi Lee

Father and Son

He has always wept and suffered without end,
He wanted just this once
To live again with his Dad
Through those pleasant childhood days
When they would walk together hand in hand,
When a warm hand used to take him to school
And he not wanting to part.
Then came the war, and the hand was cut off
Forever and ever.

The Arab boy also feels suffering,
He wanted just this once, again he wanted
To pass with his father through the same village,
The chickens clucking, the cows lowing
And the two of them happy and singing
    a lively tune...
But the war silenced the song,
A love song of a father and his son...

Amit Tal, age 11
Haifa, Israel

The Coward

You, weeping wide at war, weep with me now.
Cheating a little at peace, come near
And let us cheat together here.

Look at my guilt, mirror of my shame.
Deserter, I will not turn you in:
I am your trembling twin!

Afraid, our double knees lock in knocking fear;
Running from the guns we stumble upon each other.
Hide in my lap of terror: I am your mother.

—Only we two, and yet our howling can
Encircle the world's end.
Frightened, you are my only friend.

And frightened, we are everyone.
Someone must make a stand.
Coward, take my coward's hand.

Eve Merriam

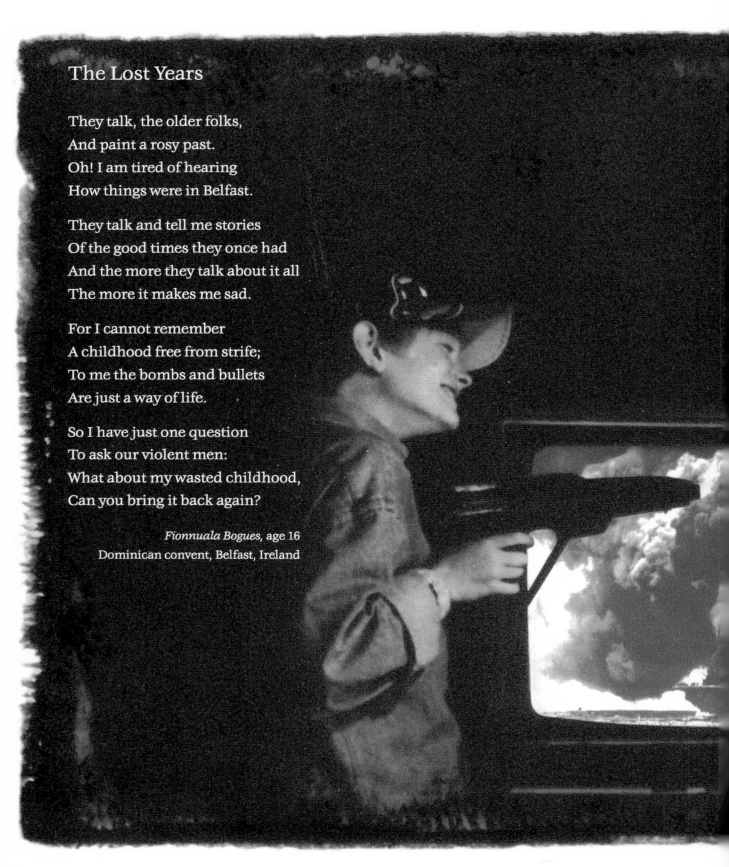

The Lost Years

They talk, the older folks,
And paint a rosy past.
Oh! I am tired of hearing
How things were in Belfast.

They talk and tell me stories
Of the good times they once had
And the more they talk about it all
The more it makes me sad.

For I cannot remember
A childhood free from strife;
To me the bombs and bullets
Are just a way of life.

So I have just one question
To ask our violent men:
What about my wasted childhood,
Can you bring it back again?

Fionnuala Bogues, age 16
Dominican convent, Belfast, Ireland

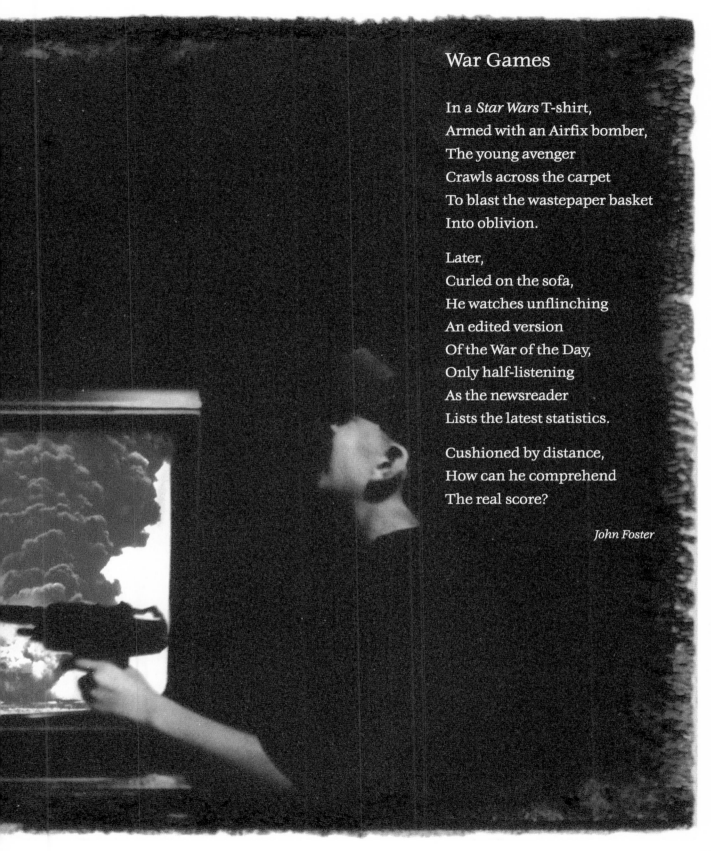

War Games

In a *Star Wars* T-shirt,
Armed with an Airfix bomber,
The young avenger
Crawls across the carpet
To blast the wastepaper basket
Into oblivion.

Later,
Curled on the sofa,
He watches unflinching
An edited version
Of the War of the Day,
Only half-listening
As the newsreader
Lists the latest statistics.

Cushioned by distance,
How can he comprehend
The real score?

John Foster

...and everywhere there shall be peace

All One People

What did Hiamovi, the red man, Chief of
    the Cheyennes, have?
To a great chief at Washington and to a
    chief of the peoples across the waters,
    Hiamovi spoke:
"There are birds of many colors—red, blue,
    green, yellow,
Yet it is all one bird.
There are horses of many colors—brown,
    black, yellow, white,
Yet it is all one horse.
So cattle, so all living things, animals,
    flowers, trees.
So men in this land, where once were only
    Indians, are now men of many colors—
    white, black, yellow, red,
Yet all one people.
That this should come to pass was in the
    heart of the Great Mystery.
It is right thus—and everywhere there
    shall be peace."
Thus Hiamovi, out of a tarnished and weather-
    worn heart of old gold, out of a living
    dawn gold.

Carl Sandburg

15

I Don't Like Wars

I don't like wars.
They end up with monuments;
I don't want battles to roar
Even in neighboring continents.

I like Spring
Flowers producing,
Fields covered with green,
The wind in the hills whistling.

Drops of dew I love,
The scent of jasmine as night cools,
Stars in darkness above,
And rain singing in pools.

I don't like wars.
They end in wreaths and monuments;
I like Peace come to stay,
And it will some day.

Matti Yosef, age 9
Bat Yam, Israel

The Paint Box

I had a paint box—
Each color growing with delight;
I had a paint box with colors
Warm and cool and bright.
I had no red for wounds and blood,
I had no black for an orphaned child,
I had no white for the face of the dead,
I had no yellow for burning sands.
I had orange for joy and life,
I had green for buds and blooms,
I had blue for clear bright skies.
I had pink for dreams and rest.
I sat down and painted Peace.

Tali Shurek, age 13
Be'er Sheva, Israel

O Mother Mine

In my dream, O mother mine,
I saw an angel with wings pure white
Breaking the rifles one by one,
Shattering to pieces each gun,
Which then into the fire he dashes
And turns smouldering ashes.

In my dream, O mother mine,
I saw an angel with wings pure white
Scattering the ashes clean
Over the glittering scenes,
And the ashes turning into a white dove,
Hovering over the east, jubilant above.

In my dreams, O mother mine,
I saw an angel with wings pure white
Lifting Moses and Mohammed
    up to the skies
And demanding they shake hands
    and be wise.
I heard his voice thunder and echo
    after them:
Quick, make haste, O sons of Shem—
Behold he is coming, the Herald of Peace,
Singing a song of praise to Peace.

Gassoub Serhan, age 14
Kfar Yafia, Jordan

One Step from an Old Dance

Will the weasel lie down with the snowshoe hare
In the calm and peaceable kingdom?
Will the wolverine cease to rend and tear
In the calm and peaceable kingdom?
Will the beasts of burden not have to bear?
Will the weasel lie down with the snowshoe hare?
Will the children feed grass to the grizzly bear
In the calm and peaceable kingdom?

Oh the wolverine will cease to tear
In the calm and peaceable kingdom.
The rattlesnake rattle praise and prayer
In the calm and peaceable kingdom.
Oh the wolves will wear smiles like children wear,
The wolverine will cease to tear,
While the hawk and the squirrel are dancing there
In the calm and peaceable kingdom.

David Helwig

The time of the singing of birds is come

The Easterner's Prayer

I pray the prayer the Easterners do—
May the peace of Allah abide with you!
Wherever you stay, wherever you go,
May the beautiful palms of Allah grow,
Through days of labor and nights of rest,
The love of good Allah make you blest.
So I touch my heart as the Easterners do—
May the peace of Allah abide with you!

Salaam Alaikum
(Peace be unto you)

Anonymous

For, Lo, the Winter Is Past

For, lo, the winter is past.
The rain is over and gone.
The flowers appear on the earth.
The time of the singing of birds is come.

Song of Solomon 2:11–12

Mother to Son

Well, son, I'll tell you:
Life for me ain't been no crystal stair.
It's had tacks in it,
And splinters,
And boards torn up,
And places with no carpet on the floor—
Bare.
But all the time
I'se been a climbin' on,
And reachin' landin's,
and turnin' corners,
And sometimes goin' in the dark
Where there ain't been no light.
So boy, don't you turn back.
Don't you set down on the steps
'Cause you finds it's kinder hard.
Don't you fall now—
For I'se still goin', honey,
I'se still climbin',
And life for me ain't been no crystal stair.

Langston Hughes

January

"Walk tall in the world,"
says Mama
to Everett Anderson.
"The year is new and
so are the days,
walk tall in the world,"
she says.

Lucille Clifton

Hope

Hope is a climber,
A brimming cup,
The elevator that only
Goes up,
A chair lift
Over the drop,
Swinging you to the
Mountain top . . .
Hope is the stretch
You make to reach
The branch that holds
The perfect peach.
Hope is a bird
Learning to fly,
Wobbling after
Many a try
Then taking off
to the giddy high,
Windy blue silk
Summer sky . . .
Hope is the moment
When you jump
Up from the tumble,
Out of the slump.
Hope is the light in the awful dark,
The clear, bright-blazing, beckoning spark
That sets your feet to a running pace
For one little look at her beautiful face.

Mary O'Neill

Birdsong

He doesn't know the world at all
Who stays in his nest and doesn't go out.
He doesn't know what birds know best
Nor what I want to sing about,
That the world is full of loveliness.

When dewdrops sparkle in the grass
And earth's aflood with morning light,
A blackbird sings upon a bush
To greet the dawning after night.
Then I know how fine it is to live.

Hey, try to open up your heart
To beauty; go to the woods someday
And weave a wreath of memory there.
Then if the tears obscure your way
You'll know how wonderful it is
   To be alive.

Unknown child
from Terezin Concentration Camp

The Sound of Machine Gun Fire

The sound of machine gun fire:
a musical air raid.
Holy visions:
bullets of caramel and ball,
a bombing attack of cookies,
pencils, colored paper,
and picture books.

A pigeon comes down from the sky,
and in his beak are the flags of all the countries.

This will be our new map,
where the trumpet sounds,
a new tomorrow for the world
while the grown-ups sleep.

Kim Yosep

translated from the Korean by Ann Sung-hi Lee

How I See It

Some say the world's
A hopeless case:
A speck of dust
In all that space.
It's certainly
A scruffy place.
Just one hope
For the human race
That I can see:
Me, I'm
ACE!

Kit Wright

A Dream

In a dream last night
I saw
The sky and earth unite.
The azure blue breeze shook hands
With the green spears.
The breath of clouds exhaling
caressed silver cheeks of rocks.

In a dream last night
I saw
The most impossible sight—
Two opposites can peacefully unite.

Anina Robb, age 16
New York, U.S.A.